D1523095

Published by Semiotext(e)
PO BOX 629, South Pasadena, CA 91031
www.semiotexte.com

Thanks to Noura Wedell, Jason Smith, Clément Ribes, David Ferrière, and Chris Clarke for their suggestions and ideas.

Design by Hedi El Kholti
ISBN: 978-1-63590-013-2

Distributed by The MIT Press, Cambridge, Mass. and London, England

jean-jacques schuhl

dusty pink

translated by jeffrey zuckerman

semiotext(e)

I'd like to achieve, one day, the dreary distant banality of those catalogs for the Manufacture française d'armes et cycles de Saint-Étienne or the Comptoir commercial d'outillage or of the *Manual of Internal Fixation* by Müller, Allgöwer, and Willeneger, or of those store windows for Borniol funeral homes (those beautiful clichés). In the meanwhile, I've copied down race wire results, *France-Soir* (in various editions), the lyrics to well-known British songs, scripts from famous old films, pharmaceutical leaflets, fashion ads, strips and scraps upon which the times are surreptitiously inscribed far better than any work of art. The rest, alas, is just me, probably.

"*Our love for brio, our penchant for virtuoso soloists, lead us to underestimate the perfection of an action that has become automatic.*"
(*France-Soir,*
8th GP sports column,
rugby game report,
France–Springboks, February 22, 1967)

"*We connect men to machines, we make new men.*"
(*Manifesto 1919–1922*
by Dziga Vertov)

"*I have taught you to hate libraries and museums . . . We are preparing the creation of the Mechanical Man with Interchangeable Parts. We will liberate man from the idea of death, and hence from death itself.*"
(Marinetti, *Technical Manifesto of Futurist Literature,* 1912)

There are sudden things:

THE BOOTS

The riot cops wear boots. They're made of black leather with laces and double straps. They're ankle height. They bulge at the instep. Near-exact copies can be found at DELICATA BROTHERS ORTHO-PEDICS, 84, boulevard Saint-Germain, Paris.[1] They don't belong to the sentries; they're loaned by the State. 23,000 identical pairs of boots that don't belong to anyone = 23,000 times more rounds of outfitting and simultaneous deployment[2] (they're deployed by the State, itself deployed according to

1. Where the always-striking window display seems rarefied in its baroqueness, tidy in its eccentricity, and somewhat anodyne.
2. Deployed among us, in the streets we walk every day, they bear on their bodies, as if sacrificed, the visible markers of a violence we give and receive at every moment and of which we are scarcely (re)cognizant.

social class), and this seemingly remote- controlled stride of mediums. Their strength (or their weakness?) and their beauty come from someplace outside themselves, from a great distance, from other people, from everybody. Leaning—in twos or threes—with Gauloises at their hips, against their impenetrable[3] gray and white Land-Rovers emblazoned with their cities' coats of arms—an abandoned transistor on the hood, which might emit a Mozart serenade that mixed with static, hissing, distant voices, from down in the police stations or the central police headquarters, curt numbers barked out from walkie-talkies into the tender, artificial—indeed, feigned—night, they wait, immobile and mute, for other groups (which also wear boots when they're not shod in athletic shoes, whether Puma [three black stripes] or Adidas [two blue stripes], and sing—HOP HOP HOP HOP HOP—and dance, with a strip of lemon-scented gauze in their mouth [can't climb up any higher, can't guess what any of them have in their heads. No idea what faces some of them hide behind their visors and others behind handkerchiefs or scarves. Down-to-earth boots matter more. Their infrequent procession repeated incessantly—it's with one's feet, after all, that one dances]).

---

3. As impenetrable as a strongbox or a pissoir.

There's a minuscule point where they intersect, and I'll circle around this point without ever being able to name it. (At the moment when the riot cop throws the cobblestone back with one hand—just one—sheathed in a two-strap mitten like the ones hockey players wear on the ice, he replays, step by step, the gesture enacted by the one who had thrown it at him.) Combat creates a space of exchange where enemies intertwine. The armor and shields of *Alexander Nevsky* and the spears of Paolo Uccello's paintings evoke—no matter what side they may be on—*something else.* At the moment they trade blows, slowly advancing and retreating in their inhuman and communal finery, the riot cops erase the something else *and are* that something else. Their appearance in the streets, as much an act of resistance against authority, stirs up the turmoil of the cruel and impersonal world of which they (fore)*tell.* There are strange complicities between enemies: Winter 1970. It's nighttime. Marie-France (in the civil registry it's Mario)—emerald-green boa, sequined black velvet gown, rhinestone necklace—leaves, in full splendor (but quite pale), the Paris police headquarters where she had been brought in to verify her identity. She had been at the club on the rue Princesse. Enter plainsclothes policemen. Floodlights. A policeman steps forward: "Put your hands over mine. When I pull back my right hand, pull back your right hand, my left hand, your left hand." They do so for a few minutes. "Your reflexes are too slow. We're bringing you in." And then in the offices:

"What's your name?"

"Marie-France."

"Don't give me that bullshit, You want me to knock you into next week? Now, your real name?"

"It's in my papers." (Subdued, drawling voice.)

A   (I nearly put the word drab, or maybe gray, here. But that would have been incorrect because in this office at the police headquarters— *at that moment*—all that's left is what's between people: things. And from the point of view of things, a police officer is as good as a flashy cross-dresser, a decrepit inkwell, a diamond necklace) officer yells as she walks away: "Good-bye, Mario (stress on the *Ma*).[4] Marie-France (who the criminal records service has already photographed several times): "Can't I get another photo?" (Subdued,

---

4. Marie-France is exterior to her voice, like Joan Fontaine in *Blackmail*, Hitchcock's first talking picture where he dubbed over her with someone whose voice bore no relation to Joan Fontaine's body, resulting in the same sort of confusion as when a famous American actor's voice generally attributed to a French dubber's voice is suddenly heard from the mouth of another (second-rate) actor, thereby making the former a bit the latter, endowing the lesser one with a glimmer of the other's celebrity.

drawling voice.) She sleepwalks down several steps, with weary, knowing grace (weary, knowing grace: these three words, assembled thus, are ones I've read somewhere, and even there they were attributed to someone else. I take them and set them upon Marie-France just like borrowed clothes draped upon a mannequin. And, soon enough, I'll set them upon someone else further down. I want to wear them out.) It's nighttime. A few hours earlier, at Alcazar, she had done a (failed)[5] imitation of Marlene Dietrich with an awkwardness that verged on affectation.

SHANGHAI EXPRESS. Ext. Night

The commander behind a table.	Why are you going to Shanghai?
Marlene Dietrich–*Shanghai Lily*, her hand with a cigarette on her thigh, her head slightly tilted like Lauren Bacall ten years	

---

5. Demonstrating what she meant to imitate through her actions, and never quite succeeding, she was just a figure wobbling deep within everything she wasn't. Which was actually beautiful.

later in a scene from *To Have and Have Not* where the exact same conversation plays out except Shanghai is replaced with Fort-de-France and the commander is a Frenchman with a beret instead of a Chinese man but each time it's a commander and a cabaret singer and Lauren Bacall walks out of the hotel at the end just as Marlene Dietrich walks out of the train station.

I want to buy a new hat.

The police officer, Marie-France, and Marlene create these (artificial) nights together.

As do the walkie-talkies and shortwave radios spinning a web of voices throughout the city, voices endlessly repeating the same thing.

Spluttering, snagging, hissing voices off in the distance, in the police stations; commingled, hampered, cracked voices that were regained, repeated, half-unheard, the start of a word, that same word wiped away, apparently not heard here, received inattentively, and so: Who's talking, and to who? What if that speech was spoken into empty space?

crossed-out speech, stuttering ahead (we're bringing these guys to the station for verification.

Over.—Roger.) with crackling, snagging, something like Edison's wireless telegraphy, Radio Londres during the war

the town nine-tenths asleep and completely crisscrossed, covered, buried by this web of waves, a crisscrossing-burial in which our gestures, our words, our intonations are inscribed, from which they slowly emerge, through which they are sometimes—more and more often—named, indexed, filed somewhere, alphabetically or by subject matter, among millions of index cards

distant voices over there, maimed voices, broken voices, spluttering or hissing as they were at the beginning of wireless telegraphy or with the first optical sound of talking pictures, a thin thread of a wounded voice indicating the abrupt, violent departure of two motorcycle riders reading one of those "Fleuve noir" crime novels (Maybe *Le "Libertad" saute à Maracaibo?*) wedged right above top of the gas tank.

And it's deep within the endless span of this acoustic plasma background that the following words take place.

(Another approach to the point I make above:)

"I don't like what comes from there." (Finger pointed at stomach.)

"Then where would you like it to come from? There?" (Finger pointed at forehead.)

"No, from there." (Finger pointed back over shoulder.)

Secondhand beauty. Made out of borrowings. Out of songs, words, dance crazes. Out of fleeting necessities. Because of accidents. (Castel, winter '66: white, shaky face against a purple background. Momentary face at a nightclub. Some stranger transformed the moment he crosses the doorway and descends [much as, beyond the STYX, everyone became a shade]—And then how could I write "Tom (Dick or Harry) stepped through the door and descended" when I don't care if it's Tom (Dick or Harry), on the contrary, what matters is that it's *anybody*—bereft of his heft, making three or four calculated moves based on the latest craze, by a crowd of other people who aren't there.)

To prefer a girl with far too large knees wearing ultra-miniskirts (they're not beautiful but they call to mind what's beautiful) to one who dresses timelessly, who is perfectly proportioned: no, that doesn't depend on—how-it's-worn.

The riot cops are ruddy, dumpy, shoddy all over, sweaty, a bit cruddy and yucky. This lack of stature only magnifies their flimsy collective beauty: at any moment these scum could lose their uniforms, their Land Rovers, their boots, this magnificent deployment independently of which they were each, individually, worthless, no better than the last of all men. Riot cop: one specimen among 23,000 bearing absolutely no trace of any history other than the one unfolding that very instant—instantaneous, compact—concealing nothing yet meaning nothing else. S.K., the famous seducer, told me: "I'm not looking for affairs. What I'm looking for is immediacy."

1967: *Borrowings* come from afar to transform us: from old Egypt for the makeup and a new way for us to keep our dead and words in the microgroove hollows of wax or in modern celluloid pyramids where voices and gestures come to bury themselves; from young China: Chairman Mao's collar ("the more trouble you make and the more you make it last, the better it will be") the celebrity slowed down to thirty-six images fixed in celluloid gelatin each second, vertical and motionless, imitated by seven hundred million

Chinese: young boys and girls individually re-creating the same gesture, diligently repeating the same word, like the LP tirelessly replaying one word millions of times, a portion of an English band's refrain. Multiplicity that gives rise to deployment—23,000 pairs of boots—

Instantaneous beauty due to multiple, multiplied accessories[6]—Boots, for example. Riot cops, Red Guards, English bands.

What matters would not be singularities distinct from a common style, but the inverse: this slow slope of a uniform, this movement rippling through us, this loss of individual consciousness, this history stripped of ego, this world minus ego, an authorless gesture[7] hanging over the void and all these things that are the pocket change of death: rushed, fleeting or, on the contrary, endlessly repeated gestures, young people—two or three or five—together rather stiff and all wearing the latest (although perhaps *last*: in this word, style and death intertwine: latest in date, but will there ever be another?) obvious, small symbols as a fitting way of coming together in common spaces,

6. The same gesture repeated seven times (a gunshot between the second and third cervical vertebrae) turned Eugen Weidmann from a simple hotel-bar pickup artist to the momentary, complacent celebrity with his "Weidmann Girls."

7. Or depthless

engaging with each other, wearing a scarf, an American way of looking good while eating braised endive followed by a Regnier Crème de Cassis sundae, their arms hard at work and their eyes somewhat lost. And everything that builds up to this point full of sweetness due solely to despair.

THE FALSIES

"The Mack Sennett bathing beauty . . . I can still see myself in the line. Marie Prevost, Mabel Normand. Mabel was always stepping on my feet . . ."
(Gloria Swanson, in *Sunset Boulevard*.)

> SURGE FROM THE FUTURE

(Advertising slogan for Philips High Reliability integrated circuits.)

This mannequin's rigidity ever so slightly cracked (by spontaneous machinery), this reflexivity—accidental, automatically brought by renown (in being reproduced and counterfeited we ourselves become somewhat false), the brand of so many British youth—inherent beginning of a new man, down to his structure, his way of walking or holding his head (like a paw or a fin an animal has gained, like the first day of Pithecanthropus erectus—terrible newness)— brought forth four or five years ago without any possible reference to our words—the contents then overflowing the sentence—arrival of an unknown, abrupt, elusive music.

(Richmond, a London suburb, August '66, one of the first pop music festivals. Watching—listening attentively to The Animals, one two, three, ten girls, all the same, beautiful and harsh, brutal and dazed, and *"they are pale pink like—bubble bubble gum,"* on the shoulders of one, two, three, ten boys, all the same, with long hair, with demonstrative indifferentism. There's a group from nobody knows where. Maybe like Rome during the barbarian invasions. But here the barbarians were among us and stunningly sophisticated.)

And also at the same time this scruffiness and this smidge of bluntness that she wears with so much chilly arrogance and this resulting contrast between sophistication and wildness (become both perfect and dead) in the pale wax mannequins found in the shops of Chelsea or South Kensington, each one watching the void (not gazing into the void or looking somewhere but truly studying the void—not a great metaphysical void, a physical void. "Nature abhors a void": thus it has to be a void). And these suavely perverse, almost clinical(ly) white girls, strolling down the streets alongside people more than thirty years older (not seeing them, striding unseen past them as they sometimes look [askance and] past them), unseeing eyes, slightly mechanical gestures, lavishly outfitted *with a small flaw*, a slight imperfection— mauve stocking with a run, grease or dirt stain, cracked fingernail, one shoe in the hand and the other on the foot, and it's a slight limp—wherein the (p)light of their beauty can plainly be seen; ten yards away, people think: "two wrongs won't make a right: there's something slightly off (but what?)" as in the solution to the *France-Soir* game of spot-the-seven-errors:

1. The bystander's right jacket lapel is visible;
2. One extra button on the duster jacket;
3. The car's right-door frame has been altered;
4. The bystander's pocket has been altered (in the background);
5. The duster jacket's collar has been altered;
6. The left boy's shirt has been altered;
7. One less finger on the left boy's hand.

   Five years ago these groups surged from the future with a new pace (all they had to do was stick their hands in their jacket pockets every so often and walk with a slight upward bounce and immediately there were two jutting collarbones— try it, it's just gymnastics), slightly raffish (with a few magnificent clothes they pulled off the look of rags, tatters, cast-offs), parading through public squares this inimitable grandeur that only certain ruffians, dressed regally, could claim. There's magnificence and also—contained within—its destruction, and consequently the converse: destruction, but beautiful.

Thus unconsciously contributing to a new morphological species, very slightly distinct, only identifiable by its details, but these quiet, unnerving details (none of them wildly provocative, just subtly indicating a wholly new order of things), these small breaches betray an absolute break with the past. Now I'll talk about a particular slowness. Bodies that gleam at night, cold and slow (the slow coldness of particular young heroin addicts who could be washed-up yet still precise in their movements), lethargic and sleepwalking. Cold white slowness (or: *coldness, whiteness, slowness*). Slow in the same way they're blond, or tall, or Chinese, and if they ever make an animated gesture, it's with a slow suddenness.

At Castel, in winter '66 (some nights on the rue Princesse a new man's gold-dot-filigreed

member card flashed) the disc jockey
plays and replays every single night:

COMPLICATED

Words & Music by

NICK JAGGER
KEITH RICHARD

She looks so sim-ple in her way... She
Wo-men seem to fill her mind. And
We talk to - ge - ther and dis - cuss. She's
She knows just how to please her man ... She's

© Copyright 1967 MIRAGE MUSIC Ltd., 88 New Oxford Street London, W. C. 1.

(31)

does the   same thing   ev - ry - day___   But she's ded - i - ca -
ma - ny   men in   so short time___   But she's un - der - ra -
What is   real - ly   best for us___   She's so - phis - ti - ca -
soft - er   than a   ba - by   lamb.   But she's ed - u - ca -

- - ted___   to   hav - ing   her___   own   way___   She's
- - ted___   She   treats me   oh___   so   kind___   She's
- - ted___   My   head's fit___   to   bust___   'Cause
- - ted___   and   does - n't   give___   a   damn___   She's

ve - ry   com - pli - ca - - - ted,
ve - ry   com - pli - ca - - - ted,
she's so   com - pli - ca - - - ted,
ve - ry   com - pli - ca - - - ted,

After last verse
repeat ⚹ to ⚹
ad lib. and fade

The dance move known as the jerk hasn't yet become widespread, so everybody is forced to dance alongside the song, on its edges, turning around it, their movements uncertain, tentative.

Gold (or silver) and wiry, the (model girls') long spangled legs dance ever so slightly wrong, very lightly off (mistakes-turned-successes?), and waver. Rigorous stuttering.

Rigorous stuttering in 1928—one of those transitory moments where gestures have to be found—1928: the dawn of talking pictures. Between 1928 and 1931 there comes the most astonishing sound of all cinematography—something slightly comparable to young pubescent boys' cracking voices. And moreover, the gestures still owe something to the syntax of (theatrical) silent films; well, they no longer have any purpose because they're accompanied by sound: they've now become gratuitous and hang as if over a void. They have the beauty of someone desperately repeating the same gesture mechanically to no avail, the last scrap of a superannuated past—a legless man, we'll say, who's just been amputated, each morning jumping out of his bed or Nijinsky in his asylum reenacting the leap that had made him famous. The first talking pictures of Laurel and Hardy or *Night of the Crossroads* with this enigmatic German woman smoking "Abdullah" cigarettes while listening to the dying voice of a time-worn, trembling gramophone consequently have the elegance of some invalids: they try to go on playing the same tricks they'd learned years before although those are now drained of necessity—and made absurdly beautiful as a result.

The gestures end, speech begins: it will be necessary to find new gestures. Cinematography broadcasts a transformation that clearly occurred "in town." The birth of the talkies wreaked havoc not only on cinema, but also, probably, on the way people behaved, their skeletal structures, the bearing of their arms, the mouths of millions of people.

SHANGHAI EXPRESS. Seq. 74. Ext. Night

Marlene (Shanghai-Lily) in the uncovered portion of a Shanghai Express train car. Her face is covered by the flocked veil of her black hat. She's in close-up with a serious, ironic (sphinx-like) smile (bitterness is far behind), her hands on her hips.

There's only one thing I wouldn't have done, Doc.

Clive Brook, military uniform, cigarette holder, officer's hat. Sitting in an armchair, with the bitter and
disillusioned tone of those
who hail from afar.

What, for instance?

Shanghai-Lily and her
famous wry smile "lost on
her lips" gently shaking her
bosom to the left and to
the right as she saw it
done—as a little girl—by
those coquettes of the Mack
Sennett Comedies: Mary
Pickford or Gloria Swanson
(who, in her dotage, declared
onscreen this obscurely
glamorous line: "When I
danced in the Bathing
Beauties, I was on the left
of Mary Pickford, and she
was always stepping on my
feet"), then taking Clive
Brook's hat and donning it,
tipping it backwards slightly
with a flick of the wrist.

I wouldn't have bobbed my
hair.

And, at that moment, her hands on her hips, her fingers outspread, her palm perhaps turned outward,
her bosom leaning slightly forward, energetically
swaying to the left and to the right, Junie Astor

repeated this gesture once or twice again in 1932 in *The Swashbuckler of Singapore*, then it disappeared, most likely it was never ever seen again. No woman in the world would enact it again, it joined all those threadbare or passé clothes. Gestures have their history.

It's a song that lasts eighteen minutes. Hands rise up, not arms outstretched above the head in an ascension or a solar communion rite or some springtime festivity—as three years later—but hands rising to obscure the face, as others do with smoke. Brian Jones is sitting, cornered, he never dances. Next to him is Anita Pallenberg. They slap each other. They look like each other (they're opposites of each other). When he comes to Paris (they say that in London he lives in a former church, they say that bags of fan mail pile up there), he spends his nights at the rue Princesse club. At seven in the morning he heads to bed, having slathered creams on his face, at the Hôtel George-V— Aubusson tapestries, wainscoting, gold accents, thick carpeting, trees flush with false oranges—in pallid confinement until the evening; then he makes his way once

again to Castel with an entourage in a
murmur of furs and swirling silks draped
upon frail, anemic, furtive, ailing, worn-
out bodies with the deathly paleness of
nightbirds.

The mid-'20s? The meeting between Lenin, his
face made up and embalmed three days after his
death, and Pola Negri (*Blood and Sand*),
Valentino's widow, is suggestive: in Hollywood
the men also remade themselves with the same
collective immodesty and kept on leading false
lives. The only revolution that could have been
interesting would have been a revolution that
negated Hollywood while preserving it, overtook.
Overtaking it, not destroying it. The Soviets' flag
should have borne the standard of the hammer
and slick falsies (socialism = Soviets + electricity
+ prosthesariat) and I like these doubly artificial
children that Lenin and Pola Negri never had.
Mao Tse-tung sometimes on the newsreels . . .
only the great silent film stars were slow like
Plastic People Plastic People Plastic People (lyrics
from the Mothers of Invention)

.   .   .   .

"Strange you shouldn't know me though, isn't
it?" presently resqueaked the nondescript, which I
now perceived was performing upon the floor

some inexplicable evolution, very analogous to the drawing on of a stocking. There was only a single leg, however, apparent. "Strange you shouldn't know me though, isn't it?

Pompey, bring me that leg!" Here Pompey handed the bundle a very capital cork leg, already dressed, which it screwed on in a trice; and then it stood upright before my eyes.

. . . .

"Pompey, I'll thank you now for that arm. Thomas" [turning to me] "is decidedly the best hand at a cork leg; but if you should ever want an arm, my dear fellow, you must really let me recommend you to Bishop." Here Pompey screwed on an arm. "We had rather hot work of it, that you may say. Now, you dog, slip on my shoulders and bosom. Pettit makes the best shoulders, but for a bosom you will have to go to Ducrow."

"Bosom!" said I.

"Pompey, will you never be ready with that wig? Scalping is a rough process, after all; but then you can procure such a capital scratch at De L'Orme's."

"Scratch!"

"Now, you nigger, my teeth! For a good set of these you had better go to Parmly's at once; high prices, but excellent work."

. . . .

"O yes, by the way, my eye—here, Pompey, you scamp, screw it in! Those Kickapoos are not so very slow at a gouge; but he's a belied man, that Dr. Williams, after all; you can't imagine how well I see with the eyes of his make." [...]

The voice, however, still puzzled me no little; but even this apparent mystery was speedily cleared up.

"Pompey, you black rascal," squeaked the General, "I really do believe you would let me go out without my palate."

Hereupon, the negro, grumbling out an apology, went up to his master, opened his mouth with the knowing air of a horse-jockey, and adjusted therein a somewhat singular-looking machine, in a very dexterous manner, that I could not altogether comprehend. The alteration, however, in the entire expression of the General's countenance was instantaneous and surprising. When he again spoke, his voice had resumed all that rich melody and strength which I had noticed upon our original introduction.

.   .   .   .

I acknowledged his kindness in my best manner, and took leave of him at once, with a perfect understanding of the true state of affairs—with a full comprehension of the mystery which had troubled me so long. It was evident. It was a clear

case. Brevet Brigadier General John A. B. C. Smith
was the man . . . the man that was used up."

("The Man That Was Used Up"
Tales of the Grotesque and Arabesque
by Edgar Allan Poe.)

THE EYELINER
(the echo of fashion)

British bands are, above all, groups. They're only incidentally musicians. The music serves as pretext for making things *together*, and making things resound *together*. Things rather than sounds. They are a prelude to armed groups. In their feedback effects and amplifiers and screams (yep, woohoo, yap) and personal effects, in everything *surrounding* their music is the premonition of a splendid storm, a destruction shrouded in beauty.

Megaphones (they shout through them), long locks, black sunglasses, boots, leather gloves, dog collars, synthesized sounds, groups of five (in some military operations, five soldiers enable a formation called a "main," or hand, formation): what might be considered a style is the premonition of street fighters armed from head to toe. The bourgeoisie weren't wrong, they reacted far more violently to all this than they would to a new style that was merely cultural. All these accessories—like the cover girls' white makeup in winter '66—prophesying the dotted outlines of a violent struggle were, in a way, themselves already a violent struggle. History has so many preludes that don't look like anything. A quirky way of dancing, sometimes. Yes, here it advanced as a dance. "On doves' feet."

Flowers of decomposition: suggestion of *something else*; a style that fragmentarily suggests another world and some instruments with which to get there; the echoes of that world are gathered back together elsewhere; here (London) this style and this (life)style seem to be wholly self-contained, finished products, frosty marvels, shuttered gazes; and people who pay them no attention—who don't have the means to do so—even though they were probably their inspiration (pop fashions came from the suburbs), will fare best, perhaps, in amplifying certain echoes—in the most violent way (like an avalanche unaffected by he who screamed and *carelessly* set sound waves moving) and in also being their point of arrival—no, it's not a matter of arrival, but rather a revival; in other countries, in a slightly dissimilar way, perhaps in another sphere entirely, although there's no other sphere, there's only this one, here and now and at all times, a sphere where everything is exchanged and where everything changes; styles pass . . . in things themselves, and they're no longer recognizable: they were so soft, so at home; style, the (mercantile) style of connecting in an industry, the game and parade a society puts on can end up presaging the death thereof.

These groups make us hear electricity. They dress themselves up magnificently for that, or rather: that dresses them up magnificently. It is not they who we hear (who we come out to hear): it's the electricity, the velvet, the storm; five thousand people looking more and more like them at ever-increasing speeds, who will now be unable to bear their daily life, and who will copy both their lyricism and their witticisms.

London, 1968, the Roundhouse: it's set in a British working-class neighborhood, an old shutdown engine shed. There are still railroad tracks, girders, switches, railway signals, fences, braziers, and gleams from far-off acetylene lamps. Every Friday, Saturday, and Sunday, the best British groups come through. Pink Floyd in a huge brick room—doubtless a former warehouse—in front of a huge mirror, its only decoration, slowly and unhurriedly doing their hair in front of three or four girls (and various people)—groupies—with very white skin and very black eyelids who never smiles. They do their hair solemnly. I'm trying to pick an example; I have a vision of a matador grooming himself before his paseo in front of Ava Gardner, I muse on the high priests of ancient Egypt preparing unguents for the dead; on how a meticulousness cloaks death here and there; on a funereal slowness (the funereal slowness of these four young men doing their hair, of these young girls' eyes seemingly transfixed upon the combs, a slowness not intended in preparation for a post-graveyard luncheon; and yet . . .). But, as with all examples, these are wrong: it is impossible, as they do their hair, to forget the locomotive right next to them, and the industrial décor (neon, factory, smoke) visible at the end of the hallway. Suddenly it occurs to me that these girls must have smudged some charcoal around their eyes—an old chunk of coal coke found just outside. When they're playing, the four members of Pink Floyd look like   , yes, like four electrical engineers trying out and toying with complicated machines.

They press a button, lower a lever, deliberately and unexcitedly pull a cord, act like they're setting it up for the next group. But no, it's for them-selves. And it's only for that purpose that they're now meticulously doing their hair, as morticians prepare the dead; to make us hear electricity. One day, young women with black eyes, white skin, and faded clothes will calmly, attentively watch Electricity Board and Gas Board workers doing their hair before leaving for work. And then they'll watch them work.

They absolutely won't use their devices or this electricity to tell us what they feel. On the contrary, they serve these devices and their noises; "a machine's mere accessories, operating them simple, straightforward, easy to understand." They're merely conduits through which this electricity can reach us. This electricity and its silent, stormy roar. And certainly words as well—flourishes for electricity—that hardly belong any more to them than to the rest of us.

All this time, in the Roundhouse, fabulously elegant very young boys and girls circulate. The details differentiating each of them don't really matter; I prefer their shared indifference. The miserable genius of each one of them can go right into the trash. What is inimitable is uninteresting. Mediums laugh at genius. They—with their awkward gestures, their blank gazes—just stammer out a mimicry of what things tell them, and absentmindedly wear any and all sumptuous rags that have been blindly flung on their shoulders.

Whose words are they singing without any real belief? Nobody's. Out there, in the dwindling night set ablaze by bluish signs (SIEMENS CONTROL DATA BULL IBM COCA-COLA), the Highgate cemetery is not far off: worms must be crawling among what had once been the rotting remains of Karl Marx.

ALL THIS TIME,
NOT FAR OFF ...

... BIBA , KENSINGTON
HIGH STREET

Facing this butcher shop there aren't any windows or store signs and this huge, somewhat caved-in opaque glass window gives the impression of an oceanographic garden, or a natural-history museum, or a mineralization and paleontology display like Nérée Boubée & Cie., or one of those fairground attractions like a Funhouse Mirrors or Haunted Maze, or a place that isn't wholly human. It's a terrible surprise to go through the door and see these soft colors, and also that massive central hallway, these terrifyingly high ceilings with light filtering through, and a total absence of clothes prolongs our uncertainty—is this even a store? Is anything bought or sold here?

Or am I on the other side of the mirror? Has the mirror closed in around me?

Who is this girl slowly making her way here with a huge dog on a leash? No signs, no salespeople, no "men's department" or "women's department," no arrows, no prices, no "sold" stickers, no labels, everything seems to be part of a system I cannot understand, a rigorous system—that of casinos, grand hotels, religious rites, factories, hospitals, stock exchanges, film shoots as slow and soundless as those cinematographic projections from before 1929—that presides over a funereal softness: that of W. A. Mozart, that of silent film.

Here, beyond the doorway, ugly women almost seem beautiful. It's a mausoleum, deep within an immense pyramid (Cheops or something like that) with its twelve (yes: twelve) colors both deathly and yet soft and sometimes ever so slightly gay: brown, black, dusty pink, gray, dark turquoise, bilberry, rust, yellow, cream, honey, bottle green, in which everything is tinged: trash cans, the beautiful salesgirls' skin (made up in those tones), stockings, hats, wallpaper, satin cushions, satin shirts, crepe dresses with leg-of-mutton sleeves, hotel-front-desk phones, and so on: trash cans are as good as pale skin, in that room in the central police headquarters as well as in the gloomy retinas of today's gum-chewing teenagers. Here, colors win out over humans.

Here, beyond the doorway, ghosts rise up to meet one another. By the shoe racks—an illusionist's box full of innumerable mirrors—it's possible to happen upon girls with faded, learned charm as they stand in the most naturally odd postures—compulsory figures—like in a game of freeze tag. The voice of Jimi Hendrix—dead eight days earlier—reverberates throughout:

"Oh, there ain't no life nowhere."

The salesgirls keep on gliding unperturbed, meticulously powdering their face, doing their hair, gently answering without ever advising, without ever sharing their opinion (this is the only store where the salesgirls also serve as models).

"Oh, there ain't no life nowhere."

A girl is standing on one foot (in a mauve boot), the other foot raised (in a black boot); another advances then retreats
    advances then retreats
    advances then retreats
    advances then retreats
    advances then retreats
facing one of her thousand reflections or reflections of reflections.

(53)

"Oh, there ain't no life nowhere."

Only cemeteries are so sumptuous and so gloomy at the same time. The mausoleum of Lenin? The tomb of young Akhenaton—just seventeen years old? I'd like for Biba to collapse and bury these fine British people with skin so pale and so pink that amid the rubble only small fragments might be perceptible: a bracelet, a shoe's toe, a closed eye, a clenched fist, a forearm, that they might be seized by death here in their freeze-tag-frozen figures, one of them half undressed in a fitting room, one with a hat in her hand, another with a hat on her head, that they might not be anything more than smudges of color
: brown, black, dusty pink, gray, dark turquoise, bilberry, rust, yellow, cream, honey, bottle green buried in the rubble where the detritus is strewn across coats and jewelry, like Bérénice Maranhão, that young seventeen-year-old Brazilian woman from a photo published in *France-Soir*: dead in an earthquake, only two thirds of her face visible, but beautiful all the same, joists and debris forming her hat; the music still enveloping them all, connecting them to things that aren't there (the butcher shop facing the store), connecting them to each other—a weak link—all now dead, the turntable still turning

(54)

and turning without anybody to listen—all these eyes wide open, calm, and dazed—like those of mannequins (nobody was ever able to perform that beautiful and furtive and simple act of using their thumbs and forefingers to shut their eyes)

Then blue turns to gray
blue turns to gray
And try as you may

or indeed

Have you seen her dressed in blue?
Oh la la oh la la oh la la la la

A salesgirl-model has dumped an entire container of "dusty pink" powder on her face: she's nothing more than a pink plaster cast now. Let this place be nothing more than a trash heap where pastel-toned junk reigns. Let the high-fidelity stereo turntable keep on singlehandedly spitting out violins, dulcet choirs, a hoarse voice

There ain't no life nowhere

something fragile and synthetic

Did you hear about the midnight rambler?
Talkin' about the midnight gambler.

I spent hours in this Kensington High Street store. Now I think I know what I was doing there: I was waiting for it to collapse. I was waiting for it to collapse upon these elegant anemic girls I'd never been able to play this game in which tenderness intertwines with death. Speaking of which, who exactly planted a bomb there four months ago that completely destroyed an entire department while leaving no victims?

ONE NIGHT
IN ANOTHER TOWN ...

The taxi stops in front of
the hotel and immediately a
d o o r m a n — s o m e w h e r e
between Emil Jannings of
The Last Laugh and Oliver
Hardy in a film where he
parodies Jannings and
opens a taxicab door in
which Jean Harlow's dress
gets stuck—bursts through
the revolving door, takes off
his hat and quickly runs his
hands through his hair,
then opens the car door and
Marlene Dietrich steps out.
The doorman bows and she
walks to the revolving door,
which a bellboy on the
other side starts turning
slowly and in this way she

enters the Friedrich II hotel, Friedrichstraße 84, Berlin, the very same one where Goebbels held his press conferences, where F. W. Murnau (*Nosferatu*), notorious for wearing a white shirt and a surgical cap during film shoots, returned for several months before his strange death in Tahiti, where asylum was found in 1944 for several Prussian countesses, refugees from the Sigmaringen Castle, and several German officers under candelabras and half-lit hanging chandeliers, the hotel's right wing caved in by bombs, the cellar full of caviar, wine, salmon, she proceeds to the reception desk, asks some questions, and then turns to make her way toward the elevator and disappears.

She exits the elevator on the fifth floor—the hallway is full of photographers, reporters, girls wearing blue jeans, louts in T-shirts (wars and the advent of pop stars have wrought havoc on the serene façades of grand hotels)—she knocks on a door that opens slightly, here she is in a countershot in the half-open door: inside are five of the Rolling Stones before their concert. One of them opens his mouth Marlene Dietrich replies and the five young stars all turn their heads toward the bygone star.

Who is it?
Marlene Dietrich

What she and they weave together with two or three wholly banal sentences far surpasses the mere words themselves.

Above all, it's the fact that *she* has come, and it's this meeting between two crumbling worlds: hers—the Berlin of 1925—and theirs—the London of the '60s—and in both is that mixture of obsolescence and violence, waste and decay in all its forms. And this as well: with her presence, she confers upon them her glory and all that she represents, they now have something of Marlene—who doesn't have much more than and is just as bereft as a call girl these days—they don't have a shared language, they repeat what they heard five minutes ago. Marlene repeated what von Sternberg had told her to say just five minutes earlier.

Events of all sorts have occurred here, and now the few words they exchange, the few gestures they make are the culmination of all that and as if nothing had ever happened anywhere at any time, as if they were (henceforth) grounded in nothing at all.

Forty years earlier she was their age, Berlin boasted the same mixture of decay, violence, and elegance as London today, and she herself was a product of that, she sang and set a trend for women's pants with all the nonchalance Mick Jagger did red lipstick or lamé boleros for men; she was also practically nothing (stars' fame are grounded in almost nothing at all), a way of saying "hello," of being just slightly aloof from her own behavior. Why has she come all this way? What has she come to find?

"Gentlemen," she said in English, and the five gentlemen turned their heads toward someone they'd heard of, someone forty years older.

there are sometimes illustrious strangers

MISS Z

Zouzou (the thin, pale, distant, smirking dancer ["she's the one over there with a British-flag miniskirt, the most mini one in all Paris, when she goes to London she stays with George Harrison," declared Pariscope] syncopating her words, zazou zoulou—sophisticated savage: "I'm the spitting image of Marlon Brando"—just arrived at the rue Princesse club from the Bastille neighborhood where she sleeps during the day, descending, indifferent, spindly, those narrow spiral steps covered with garnet velvet to mimic the grand staircase at the Casino de Paris or a dangerous Snakes and Ladders [see the way she walks, hear the way she talks]) is slight.

MISS Z II

her lower eyelashes (and rings beneath) as if
sewn on

her nose as if broken

her mouth as if painted (or grafted)

MISS Z III

strings and clips connected to electrodes are
attached to her wrists and ankles for ninety minutes
(fragile and synthetic)

MISS Z IV

yeah yeah yeah yeah yeah yeah

FRANKENSTEIN-THE-DANDY

I'll use this phrase because, first, the one I'm foisting it upon seems artificial, second, his rigidly elegant system surrounds a wound[8] like a broken

---

8. Inhuman ("I'm the girl of the year 2000," Luna declared more than a million times in a statement accompanying her photo on the cover of *France-Soir*, issue 8217) black models (their *noms de guerre* Donyale, Luna, or Kelly) in the cold of winter, 1967, came to Castel's each night, their upper and lower eyelids painted white. In May, 1968, so as to avoid crying from the gas, a tract from the Movement of March 22nd suggested putting baking soda diluted in a little water around the eyes: that was exactly the same makeup the cover girls from the previous year had worn. "Ladies, this year's battles will give you a mask that's absolutely Elizabeth Arden—deathly and sweet."

This forced elegance, produced by accident, also existed elsewhere:

France-Soir: "Ho Chi Minh's body is on display in a glass case. The President is laid out on purple velvet, his head resting on a white cushion. He is dressed in his legendary jacket. At the bottom

limb supported by the laborious interplay of straps, bandages, plaster casts, screws, splints, and pulleys. But it has to: each of his acts is clear-cut. A girl says to him one day: "It's like you're remote-controlled." When I first met him he was prone on a couch—surrounded by people—and seemed to be in a cataleptic state (His Magnetic Quasi-Catalepsy), then he had a blazer on his shoulders and a staid side-part in his hair, and these days he's got the latest looks and long locks: *the automaton's hair is far longer.*

He-the-Dandy and Z-the-Dancer bring together, in a single special moment, the most *à la mode* sophistication and the most fashionable looks, as well as a bit of the Marseillais pimp (thug) and the Bastille slut. The two both seem to pronounce words that they hadn't "found on their own," they had been whispered to them and they do not realize

---

of the bier, *the President's sandals, made from a piece of tire rubber and four strips of rubber cut from an inner tube* have been installed like a relic in a glass box."

France-Soir: "Teenagers in northern Vietnam collect the six fins of US cluster bombs and make hair-rollers out of them."

Or even this story, which was completely made up:

Tebaldi sings *Aida* at the Metropolitan Opera in New York. As the only one who could see a killer brandishing his gun in one of the luxury boxes, she lets out a shriek to attract attention. This results in the most beautiful high C of her career: everybody stands up in applause. The gunshot resounds completely unnoticed: elegance always hovers perversely over the exception that proves the rule..

what they utter. All this gives them this slightly synthetic appearance.

Useful to evoke in his case are Doctor Gibaud's mannequins, who are the centerpiece of an ad for trusses and some of whom slowly turn on their pedestals in pharmacy windows (left arm right wrist left leg right ankle wrapped in Velpeau bandages).

Or the human-anatomy or Chinese-acupuncture models whose bare bodies are riddled with dotted lines and numerals.

Or even detailed beef-cut charts.

Frankenstein-the-Dandy:
gives the impression of having always had a particular vision of himself
gives the impression of absolutely unshakable self-assurance despite being rooted in something fragile

fragile and splendid

he's been ruined. He displays this ruination

coldly exhibits his distress, outfits it in elegance and, torn between frantic modernity and some manner of evangelical morality, seeks out a state of saintliness
his taste for graves, car junkyards, as well as for luxury (Cannes, Le Mans, gold, and girls): what he

loves most about the funereal is the ceremony. Does he prefer a Lamborghini, that car akin to a flying saucer, or a Lamborghini carcass? An Ava Gardner or an Ava Gardner carcass? It depends on the day. Or rather: what he likes in a Lamborghini or an Ava is the carcass they promise.

He does his hair, pulls his jacket or his scarf on or off the way one throws a flower into a still-yawning grave.

Winter 1966: he bangs on 1.5-meter fuel canisters from the rubbish pile with a garlic pestle, standing on a platform that makes a full turn every ten seconds, his clothes covered with multicolor bulbs blinking on and off every three seconds. When he's asked what he's doing, he answers: "rubbish." Everybody knows that phrase: "it's rubbish" which falls somewhere between "it's just hot air" and "it's just make-believe." Which is Frankenstein-the-Dandy. Although it should also be said: everything in and around him is rigorous.

He depends upon an accessory, or, rather: everything within him arises from and centers upon an accessory that he wears like a mask to hide an eye injury (*the fakir's eyes have been modified*): a banal pair of tinted glasses that—as legend has it[9]—he never

9. Just like Ho Chi Minh with his jacket.

takes off. The frames are gray. After so many years of this, what he says has no meaning left, the words he utters are mere things, his sentences imprint themselves in space like comic-strip speech bubbles or foreign-film subtitles: he gently sets them all around without ever quite believing them. Even "hello" is an opaque thing belonging to someone else (some other people) who isn't (aren't) him. Belonging to the night.

The tinted glasses of a medium. The words of a medium who doesn't think what he says. Doesn't think anything at all.

I think about him—and his city (Marseille): he seems bound to that place much like a shifty presence in a familiar space, like Mandrake, the Phantom, or Fantax stuck to the streets where we make our way each day. Is this due to the oddness of a rather British comportment, clearly, impeccably rarefied, in a Mediterranean body and setting? (His Immobile Theatrical Coldness.)

And I also used these three words (Frankenstein-the-Dandy) because he exudes such everyday heroism in living like a latter-day legendary (or rather a catechismal) figure without actually succeeding, in fact remaining quite shabby in a way, somewhat lame to be honest.

Each section of his body seemed so precious to him that the least alteration would open up a chasm. In order to go unnoticed, one day he settled on moving the part on his hair from one side to the other, a detail that was as unnoticeable as the differences to be spotted in *France-Soir*: *One less black screw on the periscope – The mouth on the mask has been altered – The left-hand man's left shoulder is higher.*

COMPOSITE PORTRAIT
OF MUTANT 66

THE ELECTRIC TEENAGER

A. THE GAZE.

There's no intensity, only a prodigious indifference. The teenagers' democratic gaze (impassively
nonhierarchal: all is equal): what might be called
their nonchalance or their utter apathy. A gloomy,
contemplative mood, not at all critical, but also:
attentive to everything, the eye deeming everything
intrusive, thereby providing marvelous distrac-
tions. The beautifully glassy gaze of some gum
chewers (and Doric Adonises). His attentive gaze
lingers indiscriminately over things wholesale,

without any deference to his own concentration, but when you look at him, he is a compact, singular, inert, distinct object. He's a thing.

B. THE GAIT.

Both bouncy and clumsy. Dragging feet tracing commas. Of someone with a cracked femoral neck. That's it: a cracked gait. Hip inflexion (always the same).

He puts one foot forward and his whole body tumbles after his foot, and the whole world after his body, while he determinedly eats a Grand Marnier crêpe folded into fourths and balanced on a tiny silvery cardboard plate that he holds in the hollow of his palm.

C. THE VOICE.

It's low and bitter.

The words come from far off, from some unknown dark depth, opening cracks wide, and all this time, them, unfailing, very simple, banal, inscribed in space—like those of comic strips or photonovels.

White veiled voice.

His voice at five o'clock in the morning, which grows noticeably hoarser as the hours go by, as the whiskies go by, and then veils itself and goes white.

D. SOME STANCES.

Accompanied by: thin wordless stooped girls.

Unconcerned gestures of impeccable precision.

The index finger adorned with a huge ring has its nail ripped out almost by the root.

He doesn't strip himself of anything. He becomes bare by dint of the finery he has made his own. DISTRACTEDLY. Simplicity is never a result of overcoming complexity; rather, it's an indirect victory. He goes far off to look for himself (and never finds himself).

The club on the rue Princesse, 1966:[10] he drinks, he's quiet, he flies into fragile shards. When

10. The club on the rue Princesse, fall '66: from a specific, oblique angle his skin is tanned and his back stooped, but when seated all that is barely visible and he dissolves among these half-dead (as in this space spoke of, no longer earth but not yet the   of the dead) whose outlines are hard to make out but whose movements are in sharp focus. Earlier, he'd looked like this bat skeleton spread wide and mounted in a glass vitrine at Nérée Boubée & Cie MINERALOGY PALEONTOLOGY PETROGRAPHY MICROSCOPY HUMAN AND ANIMAL ANATOMY ZOOLOGY & BOTANY TAXIDERMY, 6, place Saint-André-des-

he gets up and walks, he seems ghostly. Soon Anita consoles him, tells him: "   ," and, amusingly, kisses, caresses, kisses the stone set in gold he wears on a chain around his neck. There's no longer any grief or feeling, only gestures, the wind outside, the countryside. What's remarkable is the spot where his shoulders meet his torso, in its fragility, like that of a skeleton, as solid as that as well, and the foreboding of something vertiginous. Only Egypt's statues could so perfectly depict a joint's combination of awkwardness and harmony. No: the word harmony doesn't work. Better to say that this awkwardness becomes self-

---

Arts, Paris V^e, with his glum gaze—is he gazing?—turned toward this suite (procession?) of dancers so focused on modern dance's frivolity: the rock steady (five positions made by rocking hips, stepping side to side, thrusting chests backward, holding forearms up, pointing thumbs upward),

the monkey, the shake (somebody giving directions out loud—eventually through a megaphone: the third, the fourth, turn around, Ray Charles, the hitchhike, the well) toward these friezes of girls with their hair pulled back Egyptian-style (just like those ads for MILA skincare products, "medical research just for your looks"), so serious, so frivolous, apparently working at a game (twinkle twinkle little girls twirling intently—much like sticking one's tongue out during a writing assignment or punishment where you have to copy these words a hundred times—a hashish cigarette, and these pink-white, pink-beige, sand-pink, pale blue stockings are the bandages of these mummies bound with slim golden belts).

evident, is banal. Asceticism or magnificence? There's no saying whether he goes quickly or slowly. If he runs he immediately ends up in a space that, despite appearing accessible to us, as real, as ordinary as any other, he alone can reach. All things considered, his proportions seem to be those of an ordinary model. Well?

A whole story bound up in a stance.

Going past the window displays at the Place de l'Opéra in Marseille—out of a jukebox wafts a bar of Donizetti while the whores do their business—he and his sister, ageless, heightless, colorless, single-file, frozen-moving, like Pharaonic couples, their feet flat, their arms against their bodies, the palms of their hands facing outward.

Thin, mischievous, and sad—in gait and face—if he moves he does so almost regretfully, yet with his whole body, but deep within lies the shadow of all the movements he left unfulfilled. And did fulfill (maybe it's better to write:) he fulfilled what would always be unfulfilled.

He hangs with good-for-nothings. So much the better. Nobody has to answer him because he immediately grabs and hoists all things, all people and all the time, up to his level and his charm redounds upon everybody around him just as a leader's glory redounds upon his soldiers and as it's clear that everything is reminiscent of Federico da Montefeltro (and not just the characters beside him on his chariot, but even the cobblestones, the lake, and the nearby hills) in Paolo Uccello's heraldic scene beneath which this inscription can be read: "He rides illustrious in glorious triumph, he whom, as he wields the sceptre with moderation, the eternal fame of his virtues celebrates as equal to the great generals."

He is sixteen years and three months old.

What is this round, prominent bone beneath the neck called?
SALTCELLARS (anat., *informal Brit.*), indentations in the shoulder, protruding features, muscle fibers, tendons, neck muscles, ligaments.

(Go to the Maloine bookstore[11] to consult a manual of bone prostheses. Read Darwin.)

He's able to make nothing out of something.

E. SOME ADJECTIVES TO SLIP INDISCRIMINATELY HERE OR THERE: hollowed, twisted, suave (irony), secret-flippant-hard, morosely pink, spidery, attentive, concerted, measured (pace), different—indifferent, painstaking

F. REMARKS.

"He himself is just a piece of machinery deep within machinery. That which is 'human' hardly interests him. Very quiet, very withdrawn, barely speaking, enigmatic, never joking, meticulously doing all he is meant to do."

(*France-Soir* on cosmonauts.)

---

11. Biba, Boubée, Délicata, Maloine: these four stores I mention here and find so surprising are places that don't look like much and which I've walked past many times without looking twice. Unremarkable façades, unexciting, even deadly boring window displays.

"A perfectly conditioned robot soldier."
(France-Soir.)

oh you the most replaceable of all beings.

finally there are the rolling stones who on themselves and around themselves call forth all these at the same time: the policeman, the cross-dresser, the dancer, frankenstein, the dandy, the robot

AT THE MUSIC HALL, LAST NIGHT

A TOAD-EATER DRESSED BY SCHIAPARELLI

Garbo-style hats, white satin peignoir, sealskin coat worn over white T-shirt, huge tinted glasses, round, red-rimmed, white foundation, black-and-gold-lamé bolero jackets, brooches, scarves, all sorts of scarves, knotted scout-style, into bow ties, into frills, ANY WHICH WAY, rings, jockey shirts, lace shirts, clown shirts, red fingernails, concealer, chintzy necklaces, mauve boas, mismatched socks, tightly tailored suits and ties, a steel chain designed like a garland, king-size cigarettes, Indian hemp powder under fingernails, swastikas on armbands or from neck badges, each one layered lightly on the last, like a sheet over a ghost, almost casually, just by chance, and also words and sounds like so much other finery enveloping them. Behind all that is nothing. It's empty. ANYBODY could do likewise.

The proof: they fly into Stuttgart with everyone in their entourage (about twenty of them); the photographers, unfamiliar with their faces, photograph everybody except them.

Models, marionettes, they betray—Frankensteins—their manipulators: they turn an entire society's violence back upon itself; they reveal it and outwit it, defy it with their own weapons, the ones society put at their disposal: the coal mines that provide electricity, the Manchester cotton mills that provide clothes. These coal mines and cotton mills end up in their songs. All England's coal, all its industrial riches, have created these five fragile people covered in silks, satins, and velvets, and this hum of electricity that will turn against it.

The rolling stones' music is the music-of-an-advanced-industrial-society and *because of that* it is its subversion, the visual and acoustic record of its magnificent deterioration.

Rolling stones:

1. Gather no moss;

2. Make fleeting noise of beautiful savagery;

3. Sometimes upset others in a rock slide and transform the earth.

The best photograph of the rolling stones (common noun, even the name of a thing), a word with nocturnal brutality reminding me of the Thames at Waterloo Bridge or Chenny Walk, the Battersea Power Station, bad boys' fights and rites— a word, really, that once pronounced leaves an aftertaste in one's throat of knives, bottle shards, soot, and wastelands—Christopher Marlowe dueling and drinking in cabarets, Cyril Tourneur raping and killing his daughter in a cemetery, and the Thames again, churning (rolling) tons and tons of spices, cotton balls, and drowned people of all colors, Thomas de Quincey eating opium, Oscar Wilde in November, 1895, standing on the center platform of Clapham Junction in convict dress,

and handcuffed, all a mannered violence, still would
be similar to those things
that appear from time to
time on page 2 of *France-
Soir* under Mlle Simone
Baron's fashion section:
Ladies Only: all five of them
would be photographed
from afar, in a long shot
without any (field of) depth,
with lines drawn from each
of their outfits, their eyes,
their cheekbones, their hair,
and their lips to a legend
outside the image listing the
source, the price, the specifi-
cations for the clothes
worn, as well as the product,
its price, the store where
ANYBODY can buy these particular beauty and cosmetics
products for their faces.

This would very nicely
show their quality as inter-
sections of things, as stan-
dard-bearers unencumbered
by standards, of mere things
among other things—their
hair is simply a product.
The photograph would ultimately be literally eroded
(their faces would ultimately

be eroded) by this heap of
lines and legends such as:

Orlon Mascara Eyeliner,
30 Francs

Crushed Velvet Jacket,
45 Pounds Sterling, John
Crittle & Co, 161 King's
Road, London, SW3

Socks, Prisunic, 8 Francs

Geometric Anti-Fatigue
Glasses with Tinted Lenses,
120 Francs, Simon of New
York

Movers' Leather and
Copper Wristbands (Amsterdam Flea Market), 45 Francs
sometimes slightly impin-
ging upon them (cutting
into them) so that all that
can be seen are snippets
through the words and
numbers.

I've forgotten: maybe a
few strikethroughs could be
overlaid upon all that (it's
more or less the same)

When Mick Jagger
(high priest flanked by four
sleepwalkers), in March '67
at the Olympia, came back
out one last time to sing
having (been) draped (with)
a white satin (or maybe it

was silk) peignoir upon his shoulders, he wore onstage what would normally be donned backstage. (He brought backstage onstage) like someone in a rush to do away with his artifice and give us some insight into how he lives, not how he is, much like those blues singers finally sharing their supposedly private lives with the public. With this peignoir he showed us that he, like us, was just a succession of façades, each one equal, and that all around was the void (that abhors nature). Singers almost always impoverish themselves over the course of a performance to reveal their heart to us: they send away the other musicians, break their guitars, rip off their shirts, and think they're stripped bare.

I dream of a performance where the inverse obtains: tons of people and accessories would gravitate all around the celebrity until she or he, dressing up with all the studied, awkward slowness of a Pigalle striptease dancer, would have no other option than to disappear for lack of any further space; everybody would end up watching a reverse striptease, far graver and riskier than its inverse: we have to accumulate wealth and disappear from sight beneath all our riches.

Mick Jagger's white peignoir is the first (mis)step toward a world where things would always be there, each one equal, and not always elsewhere, hidden (and to begin with: hospitals, factories, cemeteries always kept exiled from towns and yet the be-all and end-all of everything).

Given that at the very moment he reveals himself he conceals himself. And vice versa ad infinitum. He frees himself up as he weighs himself down.

Ooh-ooh Ooh-ooh (in unison) Yeah, Yahh, Hip, Hop, Ooh, Oh yeah yeah oh yeah yeah, fingers snapping, hands clapping, doors slamming, windows cracking, unidentified noises: things speaking without interference

Wafting their cruelty on bars of degenerate fados or on a fifty-violin accompaniment (seeded with disused and dated embellishments) and mixed choruses—but there are fifty policemen around

The rolling stones' song is between them and us, it doesn't belong to them

What they borrow from old England: a Lady Windermere's Fan look, completely Establishment —they sing at the Royal Albert Hall—mother-of-pearl opera binoculars. All this slightly, *distinctly* at a remove. Top hats. A ceremonial stiffness, but they show how all this—already at a remove—unravels. *They destroy it before our eyes*

> LEAN ON IT
> ONE LAST
> TIME

These crushed-velvet bell-bottoms, these patch-works, these long haircuts, these songs aren't the opposite of the old colonial world, but the irony, the forgery thereof.

Recently, wearing raspberry satin, pink top hats, silver lamé shirts, looking solemn and funereal, they could have been perfect mannequins for Schiaparelli. Except: the hat they threw to the ground as they walked in—that's called sparking a craze—the satin jacket was soaked with sweat and they pulled it off, the lamé shirt was a bolero and revealed their belly button.[12] They were a good dynamic measure of how much time had passed between Schiap's "postwar" and today. Ever serious, they have an immediate understanding of parody, derision, and consequently history. They are both

---

12. The singer throws back his hat, his scarf, or his hair *the way one throws a flower into a still-yawning grave.*

tradition and its destruction. They don't leap over
this tradition (they're never
straightforward). They lean
on it one last time. They
show it coming undone.
They themselves come
undone. *They have come
undone.* And we clap.

We see that they most
often perform in places that
are typically the locales for
the largest boxing matches
—Madison Square Garden in
New York (the same audience
as that for Clay–Frazier), the
Palais des Sports in Paris—
or sometimes in venues
featuring opera's baroque
architecture—the Royal
Albert Hall where *La Tosca*
occasionally sings: violence
and rococo.

TICS	TOC	TICS
TOC	TICS	TOC
TICS	TOC	TICS
TOC	TICS	TOC
TICS	TOC	TICS

Their performance,
much more than the music
hall, evoke the commingled
suaveness, tawdriness, and
aggressiveness of the bull-
fight, the sworn yet sumptuous game of Mass, the
noises and colors of a tat-
tered ritual, not mere music
but holy performance.

The singer spaces out
his gestures as a typesetter
might his words.

Nothing is more beauti-
ful than this wild crowd, this
violent whirlwind music—
and with that the singer so
slow, so mannered, like a
priest presiding over Mass,
his gestures at a remove
from his voice, his gestures
and his voice at a remove
from everything around
them, his gestures and his
voice and everything around
them at a remove from what
is outside.

They don't leave any
trace, they retain the trace of
everything.

Each note of theirs
makes us dream of their face.

With each word he pro-
nounces Mick Jagger flips
inside out like a glove. He
doesn't think about what he

says. He thinks about providing a *physical* presence to
the *words* he sings.

What do these bracelets
made of rectangular mirror
fragments reflect? Fragments
of the room? or of him? or of
the two mixed together?
Reflect thoroughly.

It is very troubling that
their glory is grounded in
nothing. It is the glory of
each one of us.

Degraded music, five-
and-dime music, garbage
music, barren music, light
night music.

Mick Jagger doesn't
stop dancing. Or vomiting
(words as well as toads), he
vomits as he dances.

The photographs where
they're dressed up as sailors,
as a circus troupe, as women:
disdain for a particular style,
identity, brand image, personality. As women: that
mockery of a specific myth
of masculinity peculiar to
the preceding generation.
Brian Jones dressed up as a
Nazi: screw our parents,
screw everybody at Yalta,
screw all humanism, long
live death. Provocation is
sometimes a way of reestab-
lishing reality.

The drummer for the
rolling stones, Charlie
Watts (as in electricity): no
more or less than a drum
major for military bands,
the riot cops, or one of
these music machines made
in Switzerland

AN ELEGANT
CONSTRAINT

Arriving at Hyde Park
for a concert in a BRINK'S-
cash-transport armored van
(their byword: speed and
security), two policemen on
the running boards, the
rolling stones suddenly look
like five million pounds sterling. Fake, of course. The
rolling stones are as beautiful as five million fake
pounds sterling.

Like all superstars the
rolling stones aren't anything
anymore: anything but us.

The rolling stones don't
serve their art. They use it

to serve what is around them: their clothes, the nightclubs, the last grand hotels, the airport concourses, the police stations. They sing for that alone. That's their song.

> BE HOLLOW YOU'LL RESONATE BETTER BE HOLLOW YOU'LL RES ONATE BETTER BE HOLLOW YOU'LL RESO NATE BETTER B E HOLLOW YO

Like all others transformed by glory, the rolling stones have lost their souls definitively: they're hollow, which is why they resonate well.

Europe 1 radio network, Friday, May 24, 1968, at night: "We could see young girls, maybe fifteen or sixteen years old, from the city outskirts, ridiculously made-up, pulling crowd-control chains to gird their loins before using them as weapons against the police." They're the same ones as—or the sisters of—those who had walked out of the Olympia one year earlier with banners reading LONG LIVE THE STONES and mischievous shrieks. That day, the place de l'Opéra was blockaded by police that charged the sidewalks in vans like Italian Celeri troops. One year later they no longer looked at the (cobble) stones, they used them. They had become weapons.

> POP POP POP P OP POP HOP H OP HOP HOP H OP

Paris, 1966–1968

A handcuff on his wrist—when Keith Richards is arrested for drugs—a bandage hand in plaster—Brian Jones—and that's one further accessory.

In the concert halls of the biggest cities, nobody hears the rolling stones: they're drowned out by electricity and crowds (all that noise for nothing). And what is heard is false (Decca stereo disc # 2580275). And what is seen is also false, awkward, artificially precise. What remains? Precisely this falseness, which deteriorates, although beautifully, sounds and postures we no longer want. Which makes the machine grate: while some shapes are smashed to pieces, a new morality is forged.

Their acts and gestures have the sumptuous, anonymous beauty of a thing belonging to nobody. Each of them, in their gleaming thinness, is there, fragile and ineluctable, solitary, devoid of all justification, having seemingly come from nowhere, leading into the void of our (non-)imitation, piece of a puzzle that doesn't exist, scrap of this heretofore completely unseen behavior that it falls upon us, now, to invent.

> AND NOW FOR THE
> FIRST TIME IN THE
> WORLD A COLLECTIVE
> STAR
> THIS IS ONLY A START
> AND NOW ONWARD
> FOR THE THREE BIL-
> LION STARS

including the disintegration of all that (it has not yet been thoroughly noted that there's tragedy in fashion as might be suggested by its fatal trajectory toward death):

THE TWO SCARVES
NOVEL

"Style isn't funny.
It's something on the brink of suicide."
Coco Chanel.

09:30 BR BR BR BR BR

14:35 1st race

protest lodged by the 2nd against the 1st

protest lodged by the 3rd against the 1st and 2nd

14:48 1st race

protest not accepted

15:14 NA   NA   NA NA NA NA

15:19 SS   SS   SS SS SS SS

Testing Testing Testing Testing Testing Testing

9 8 7 6 5 4 3 2 1 0 1 2 3 4 5 6 7 8 9

17:43 4th Kassandra Prize Derby

401	Baudelaire
402	Nonchalant
403	Only Son
404	Dream of Glory
405	Forever
406	Beautiful Evidence
407	Your Story
408	No Satisfaction
409	Let It Bleed
410	Lady Jane

18:02   Results-5th

1	Child of the Moon
2	Get Out
3	Careful Miss

19:03	7th
701	Electronic Bubble Zero
702	Mekanik

703	Très Snobe
704	Rag Doll
705	Pink and Black
706	Prancing Vamp
707	Faithfully Yours

19:50   Helena Rubinstein, the woman who made beauty a global market, has died at 94

19:51   Zürich Kloten: PFLP commando unit hidden behind snow and black coats attacks Boeing 720B EL AL runway 28

19:55   London: Brian Jones, lead guitarist for the rolling stones, has died tonight at 24
end afp end afp end afp end afp end afp

While down there, in this villa just outside London, at the bottom of a swimming pool where an inhaler lies on the edge of the concrete, his features slowly decompose and fade away, here, in this office with nobody present to witness it (someone will only distractedly walk up much

later once the wirephoto is complete and the
original no longer needs to be sandwiched), the
inverse operation begins, recomposing a face in
the manner of a puzzle or a machine that weaves
complicated patterns or even a five-cent coin set
beneath a thin sheet of paper for someone to take
a pencil rubbing
Steadily a dead man's face will appear, all alone,
first for nothing, for nobody, uncovered in the
void. At first this is only a thin black thread that
thickens slightly to the right

and in Surrey some British police officers slam the
Austin's car doors and enter the villa where a
young, sluggish Swedish girl greets them, practically sleepwalking, her voice slow (heroin?) and
her miniskirt three-quarters of an inch lower than
it had been last winter

then this black thread stops and starts but with
repeated back-and-forths (just as a face appears
beneath the water, a water that barely makes any
waves); some smudges

the coroner concludes it was death by drowning but the autopsy is not yet finished. Two policemen are on guard in front of the entrance to the "£50,000 villa" and keep the journalists from entering. It's still

this isn't anything yet but soon this will be his hair, but before that will be his eyes, and even his nose because his hair was so long

night. Really, the flashbulbs, outside, the swimming pool lit purplish-blue, this hubbub around someone no longer able to perform but still bearing the same legendary, false splendor as when he was doing so, crumbling beneath spotlights, screams, clothes—and always seemingly a stranger to his clothing—magnificent poor wobbly thing, a face that could just as easily be an archangel's as a little old lady's (or is it actually: a child in the morning, an old man at dusk?)

longer than that of the other four men

"Who is it?"
"It's Brian Jones," another British policeman replies,
you know, the biggest stoner in the rolling stones"
"Well, soon he'll be just rolling bones"

He stares straight at something in front of him
that we can't see, and a smile will come to his lips,
an odd smile (ironic? amused? sad? all of the
above? none of the above?), and here's the smile
at last

How long does it take for a corpse to start decom-
posing? It's there on the edge of the pool with its
tinted glasses and inhaler nearby (he was asthmatic,
but also having an inhaler lets him take in the
cannabis smoke more easily) and at the bottom of
the pool is the telephone

and then a window with a handle—he's in a car, and now a scarf with fringes and tassels around his neck, and another scarf beneath—all that very black, very white

the doctor is on his knees and takes some blood from the dead stone whose stupor hasn't completely vanished from his face and the young, wi(ld)ly sluggish, practically sleepwalking Swedish girl the journalists will be saying had been just a companion fixes her makeup. "The scream of the ambulance"

transmitted by underwater cables, a smile transmitted from over there by underwater cables and touching dry ground here in this empty France-Presse room (it's a photo that was taken two years ago at Zürich's Kloten airport when

the phone is now ringing nonstop in the Surrey villa

he'd come to play a concert that ended with riots in the street (how can such a gentle, wrinkled face, belonging to an ultramodern old man, ringed, ringed by wealth, or to a crabby child, set off riots?). The deep-furrowed eyes—already deathly— furrows accentuated even more by the wirephoto's contrasts

"As soon as the drowned man's body rose back to the pool surface the young, wily, sluggish Swedish woman, who was practically sleepwalking (Nembutal?) attempted mouth-to-mouth—the kiss of life."

This silence, these softly spoken words, so much precaution and precision, these few policemen standing guard, all this surrounding the death makes it reminiscent of those nighttime shoots for certain films (the best ones). These are similar ceremonies connecting the two productions. The scream of the ambulance.

The face becomes simultaneously clearer and choppier. It's cloudy. The blacks bleed. It's printed indifferently. It develops a thread the other end of which would be in the "£50,000 house," coming apart there in Surrey, creates this ethereal face that death itself is distilling here, this oval black-and-white portrait

This swimming pool—so Sunset Boulevard—(but he was just a former star because for two months now he'd just been an ex-rolling stone: in fact, maybe, given that death is never, no more than anything else, ever natural, the medical examiner and the police should have searched in that direction, maybe that's what killed him and for good reason: wanting to become an individual, to make his own music, to no longer feel four ghosts hovering around him every time he went to buy a scarf at Biba on Kensington High Street, the store that felt both like an aquarium and a bank, or had a cup of tea at Antique Market, or some whiskey at Arethusa, or coffee at Chelsea Potter, or told his driver: "Take the Iso Grifo [or the Iso Rivolta] and go pick up Miss Anita in West Berlin and bring her back here" or said—did he say it?— "hello" upon arriving at Catherine Harlet's, or when he burst in tears because he'd learned that because he wasn't allowed to visit the USA because of drugs, the group couldn't do a tour there) is deserted now, everybody has gone back into the villa (with its doors open, as always happens in catastrophes), carrying the body there, except for the two policemen, the police always more or less associated with the rolling stones (to protect them or imprison them, it's never clear which) while the ambulance parks in the garden that it sweeps ceaselessly with the orange paintbrush of its turret light, its sirens momentarily silenced. Three-quarters of an inch added to the skirt of the young wildly sluggish Swedish woman who was practically sleepwalking (she's wearing "Detchema" by Revillon) and the statistics published by *France-Soir* on September 7, 1969, show that in France skirts had lengthened by one inch, in North America by half an inch, and it was in Australia that they were shortest this year, a report from a Swiss stock broker showing, for that matter, that the market follows styles: it rises or falls in tandem with skirt lengths; the foreign exchange brokers at Harris Upham & Co. christened this metric the Hemline Index. This year has been the year without fashion, as if history had bet on absolute upheaval and recoiled in terror, afraid even of a season's fleeting fashions, of such a pale imitation of (a)history and so spared itself—none of these terribly new films, more of these tight-lipped, slightly ridiculous expressions, a fleeting season's words that only two hundred people might use but which now have to be cast into the past:

Ace (with hard stress)

Funkadelic (stress on *del*)

Coot

Pigs

reminiscent of that polite listlessness of old languages, then, in October, these fifty model girls suggesting in passing, by chance, some colors, some shapes, some steps (indecisive indices), and for a moment it's possible to envision how everything could be different. (Step back Stop The new species will never pass Stop Long live the old refrains Stop.) No one is called ANDA, BULLE, AMANDA, ZOUZOU anymore, new names with a sweet ferocity befitting computers, nuclear reactors, guerrilla fighters, or royal dynasties. People are back to being called Jeanne, Brigitte, France, we've become straightforward and eternal again. A Man and a Woman Live to Live The Things of Life

like the eyes of a funereal clown or a funereal mime-singer à la Stan Laurel or Fred Astaire, explosive cocktails of fantasy and deathlike rigidity, which gives them that gauche elegance and so now the rolling stones number not five but six: five + one corpse. They've been enriched by a great void. One more accident and since Brian Jones died they've become all the more beautiful because beauty is a sum of accidents.

There's a word for each thing, no more unintelligible void, nothing is indescribable, nothing anymore is unnamable, unfortunately I can write these lines

"I see the inside of your head, the bones of your skull, the neural circuits of your brain's lobes, the underside of your eyeballs, your optic nerve, blood all around, I have X-rays at the end of my eyes, I'm afraid," he said six years ago to Z the dancer after they took some LSD 25. "Don't leave, stay here or I'll kill myself, I'll jump out the window" (jumping out windows was his great obsession—having, in New York, been caught at the last minute on the Algonquin's balcony by his agent Andrew Long Oldham). They had been locked together for three days in this hotel room at the Commodore, scarf on the bedside lamp, incense, pitch pine and tarlatan,

Tranxene and Librium 10 galore just as, in *Sweet Bird of Youth*, Paul Newman and I don't remember which actress playing an actress inconsolable at being seen so wrinkled up close

one scarf over the other in the now-complete photograph: if something has lost its appeal, it doesn't have to be removed, canceled, instead it has to be complicated, added to, ruined. Like the ancestral generations passing through a family home again and again, keeping each thing almost religiously where it had been in this outmoded universe of ancestors' portraits and useless objects, placing a piece of furniture, a painting or oneself on top, a small detail on a gray backdrop.

For example this "£50,000 house" in Surrey neutralized by having been inhabited in so many ways, and him inscribing onto this neutrality, this overpowered, fabricated blankness that has become nothing more than a massive nonentity in the wake of so many intentions layered upon one another and canceling each other out, intersecting, altering, ultimately negating all the others, the writing of all his gestures, all his words (hello, good-bye, thank you, yes, no) multiple and complicated erasures "arriving at pure whiteness"—this bareness the final destination of so much gleaming, not at all crude but a sort of halo that hasn't stripped away anything it touched nor even diminished it as in asceticism but (maybe it's possible to write:) having unfulfilled what was not yet fully unfulfilled.

Whether he was at Castel among the velvet, the old engravings, and the rococo, sitting on a stair step, or onstage at the Royal Albert Hall, dusty and full of old gold, wainscoting, and detritus, he never changed his ways, which weren't much at all, but five thousand people congregated in front of him (them) shrieking and tapping four shorts on the ground then indistinctly yelling out two long beats—the stones—and he became famous. He summoned up a particular order of things. He wasn't "someone" (him, Frankenstein-the-Dandy, Z the dancer, the Pharaonic couple, the spidery London girls, all those merged together and if he made a single gesture, it felt to me as if everybody made it—or maybe nobody, maybe this gesture made itself. No: was made. By them all and by none at all. By everybody, obscurely) and the hat set on his poor figure like an object with no relationship to his body (but doesn't a hat always have an aspect of something autonomous, inhuman, stranded? The fact that the person wearing it doesn't see it—it's above the line of sight—gives it a a treacherous aspect).[13]

A sort of desperate chic

Living mummy (like a Peruvian mummy)

the band fell apart (decomposed beauty): it was already in their music which doesn't stop coming undone, unraveling, in their clothes which are always missing something, they're always coming undone, their beautiful undoing continues

accepting anything put on them, letting things come, compromised, not pure in the least, products, nothing more than products, from head to toe, and

---

13. Doesn't the line "keep it under your hat" have its roots in this ironic treachery always implicit in a hat?

so being there, like that, decaying yet splendid manifestations—of us all; when all five of them pose, it's clear that they didn't create themselves at all, that they don't have a personality but rather hundreds of them, which is to say none at all anymore, and that they never *wanted* anything, those idiots

today following that tradition of the great aging Hollywood stars the rolling stones decided—at twenty-five years old—to withdraw to those majestically passé villas on the French Riviera

(*France-Soir*, March 1971)

movement that's become Qulture

caption on a *France-Soir* photograph from May 12, 1970: "Saturday afternoon in Saint-German-des-Prés. Style or styles? It may never have been possible before, but now women can be chic when they wear a duster jacket, a mini-skirt, a calf-length item or even a dress from ten years ago. Nothing looks ridiculous, everything is classic. Matriarchs and schoolgirls all wear the same pants which hold no allegiance." On the back of this photograph and therefore in the same clipping is the solution to the spot-the-seven-errors:

1. The soldier's leatherwork has different outlines on its lower left side.
2. The right-hand armchair's right foot has different outlines.
3. The jacket's lower pocket has disappeared.
4. The left-hand priest's skull has different outlines.
5. The king's left sleeve has different outlines on its lower side.
6. The coat on the passerby in the background crowd now covers his left shoulder more.
7. The night horse's back-left hoof is different.

I write Brian Jones, I could write X or Y. This act is done (this word is said) through Jones (Jones: the British Dupont), X or Y. Doesn't matter. What matters is that it's done.

> *Which one of these I see is really you,*
> *It is not clear*
> ("Earth Opera" band)

secondhand rags cast-offs

impeccable macabre whiteness

> *I don't feel anything . . . and I don't feel*
> *anything . . . still I don't feel anything*
> ("Earth Opera")

Wall Street: 80 index; the dresses: four inches
above the knee

noticeable in the room where he lies and where
there floats the ghost of a dead pharaoh are:
—an AGLA automatic injector (with hypodermic nee-
dle), allowing a ±0.00005 ml margin of error in
measuring liquid volumes, and suitcases still covered
with hotel tags sometimes stuck atop one another:
Algonquin Hotel, New York (Garbo and Mae Murray
        were dining at the next table over)
Hilton Hotel, Tokyo
Embassy Hotel, Bruxelles (the couch's upholstery
        was altered)
Grand Hotel, San Francisco
Hôtel Saint-James & Albany, Paris
Albergo Principe del Piemonte, Milano
Albergo Roma e San Pietro (the walls there make
        up a snakes-and-ladders game with its

squares, its numbers, and its spiral shapes:
     Well, Prison, Bridge, Maze, Death)
Hilton Hotel, Berlin
Hôtel George-V, Paris (on the terrace where tea is
     served, there are trees with fake oranges)
Hôtel du Sphinx, Lyon

Hôtel Carlton, Cannes (the neckline shape *on the
     T-shirt is different*)
Duke's Hotel, Edinburgh (a Velpeau bandage for the
     wrist is one further accessory)

Grand Hotel Krasnapolsky, Amsterdam
King's Hotel, Miami
Grand Hôtel des Étrangers, Toronto
Grand Hôtel & Hôtel de Noailles, Marseille (that
     day he was wearing an old blue wide-
     brimmed crushed-velvet hat and his suitcases
     —the same ones now bearing the name of
     the hotel—were portaged by a gold-but-
     toned leather-booted bellboy barely younger
     than he was with his child or old lady's
     face and he was accompanied by Anita
     Pallenberg continually bearing those signs
     [wide-brimmed crushed-velvet hats,
     leather suitcases from La Bagagerie that
     smell nice and crack, winged scarab with
     dusty rubies and emeralds hanging from a

small chain on her jacket buttonhole, and
the exhaustion of a perpetual traveler⌉
reminiscent of luxury trains ⌈TRANS
EUROPE EXPRESS⌉ and grand hotels,
exhibiting a strange resemblance ⌈com-
plicity⌉ with him, the two of them sickly, a
bit hopeless, especially when eating on the
second level of the Gare de Lyon in this
overbearing, baroque décor of a suspended
cathedral—perfectly reminiscent of the
pomp and gold of the Royal Albert Hall or
the George-V—under the frescoes of those
towns the Paris–Lyon–Mediterranean railroad have made reachable: Sousse, Algiers,
the Old Port of Marseille, the Lac du
Bourget, Beaulieu, Antibes, the Lac
d'Aiguebelette, Mont Blanc, Le Loubet,
Monaco, La Meije, Hyères, Saint-Honorat)
Hôtel du Lac, Geneva
Hôtel Gonet et de la Reine, Cannes
Le Corbusier Hotel, New Delhi
Hôtel de Bordeaux et d'Orient, Marseille
Hôtel de la Presse et des Messageries, Tunis

Hôtel Mamounia, Marrakesh (with a baby in tow,
    but which felt like a film)
Hôtel Bijou Sélect, Dakar

without anybody to see them (like a newsreel and the room is empty at ten in the morning), soon there will be nothing left but a few scattered traces of his tragic, worried, outmoded, dark coquetry, for example those clothes thrown on armchairs covered with a white cloth under a crystal chandelier, JEWELS OF A CROWN FOR NO ONE, for nothing, meaning nothing (but having never meant anything),[14]

everything here now undone.

---

14. But what does the tiger, prowling, mean?

ABOUT THE AUTHOR

Jean-Jacques Schuhl won the Prix Goncourt in 2000 for his novel *Ingrid Caven*. He is the author of *Telex no. 1*, *Entrée des fantômes*, and *Obsessions*.